POP,
_ you because you
_ow to play marbles and you
_es with me. I Love You!!

Love you
Jamie
age 9

Dear Gradmma,
I love you so much because
how much you love me, because
the way you hug me tight, because
how you love me too.

Loves, Your
Grand child
Cassie
Age 8¼

Dear Granpa,
I love you because
you always let me Drive
the tractors and you
have my favorite meals
let me pick the me_
and play with the cat

Love,
_____

Dear Grandma,
I love you because you give me
things and treat me good. You are
the best.

Love,
Austin
age 8

Dear Grandad,

I love you because you taught
me how to go fishing and use tools.
Thank you for teaching me how!

Your Granddaughter,
Vicki
age: 9

Dear, gramom

I Love you because you are gratist and best gramom
I ever had. xoxoxoxoxoxo when ever I come over you are
allways their for me. when I need you!!!! I don't
no what I would out you!!!!!!!

I Love You gramom

I Love Kevin

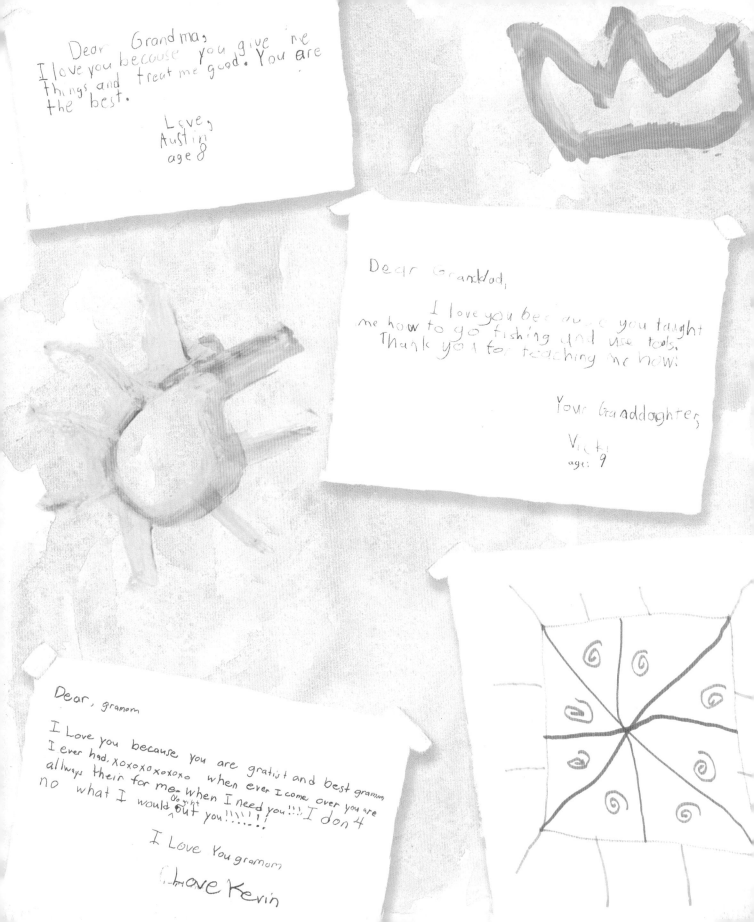

The GiFTs of being Grand

is dedicated to Grandma Mary, Nana Richmond,
Grandpa Jerry and Papa Richmond ... for being so grand! —MR

A special thank you to Ms. Megan Scully's 3rd grade class at
Bobby's Run School in Lumberton, New Jersey. Their notes
to their grandparents are a treasured part of this book.

© 2003 by Marianne Richmond Studios, Inc.

Marianne Richmond Studios, Inc.
420 N. 5th Street, Suite 840
Minneapolis, MN 55401
www.mariannerichmond.com

ISBN 0-9652448-8-1

Illustrations by Marianne Richmond

additional illustrations by
Cole Richmond, age 5 and Adam Richmond, age 4

Book design by Sara Dare Biscan

Printed in China

Fifth Printing

The Gifts of being Grand

for grandparents everywhere

by Marianne Richmond

Seems like only yesterday,
    your kids were little tykes,
climbing trees, scraping knees,
    and riding bright red bikes.

"How did all this time go by?"
    you fondly reminisce
about demanding days long gone
    and pleasures that you miss.

"*G'Bye,* mom and dad," your children now grown
said as they started living life on their own.

In time, there were houses and spouses and pets, new cars and new jobs, some savings and debts.

You wondered, sometimes, as moms and dads do
if their plans would include a couple of kids, too.

Just Married

Congrats!

Best Wishes!

Savings Acct.

Rent
Bill

TRUE LOVE

Electric
Bill

"kids change your life..."

(But you wouldn't
dare pry, 'cause it's just
not your place
to ask such questions
that invade their space.)

your child is saying you'll soon be a Grand!

"*Congratulations!*" you say.

"Am I ready?" you muse.

"You're excited?" they ask.

"OF COURSE!" you enthuse.

And while your joy may truly be true,
this grandparenthood thing just happens to you.

No classes or counseling or special instruction
for this once-in-a-lifetime grand induction.

"A Grand?" you confirm,
    and to your utter delight,
it feels quite comfy,
    so wonderfully right.

You're instantly smitten
　　with cute clothes and shoes
and everything precious
　　in pinks and in blues.

Baby Department

"*Welcome,*" you whisper
    and know more than maybe
you're head over heels
    in love with this baby.

This wee wondrous person
whom you've not met before
starts filling your life
with grand gifts galore.

The gifts of being grand
    are the gifts of much more FUN ...
the sweet rewards for parents
    whose front-line jobs are done.

Okay ... you admit
    you'll treasure that call
from your child asking,
    "How did you do it all?"

You get permission to spoil
  your grandchildren plus
a reason for silliness
  and the privilege to fuss.

Your house is for loving
and cuddling and baking,
stories and coloring
and sweet memory making.

You're a popular host
    for "you and me" playing
like field trips and shopping
    and overnight staying.

And, oh, if you could
you'd buy up that store
to shower your darlings
with cool toys and more!

All this indulging
    you'll happily do,
but the greatest of gifts
    is what they give you.

A new name for start, an endearing ID,
like Nana or Papa or Grammy or Gee.

You'll try that name on, though it won't really matter
when it's said by the one whose feet pitter-patter.

You get a (sort of) second chance.
　　You're more patient than before.
You leave behind regrets,
　　and enjoy it so much more.

"Were my kids ..." you ask, "as funny and smart
　　as these grand little people
　　　　who've captured my heart?"

They beg you to journey
through life at their pace,
discovering adventure
in the simplest place.

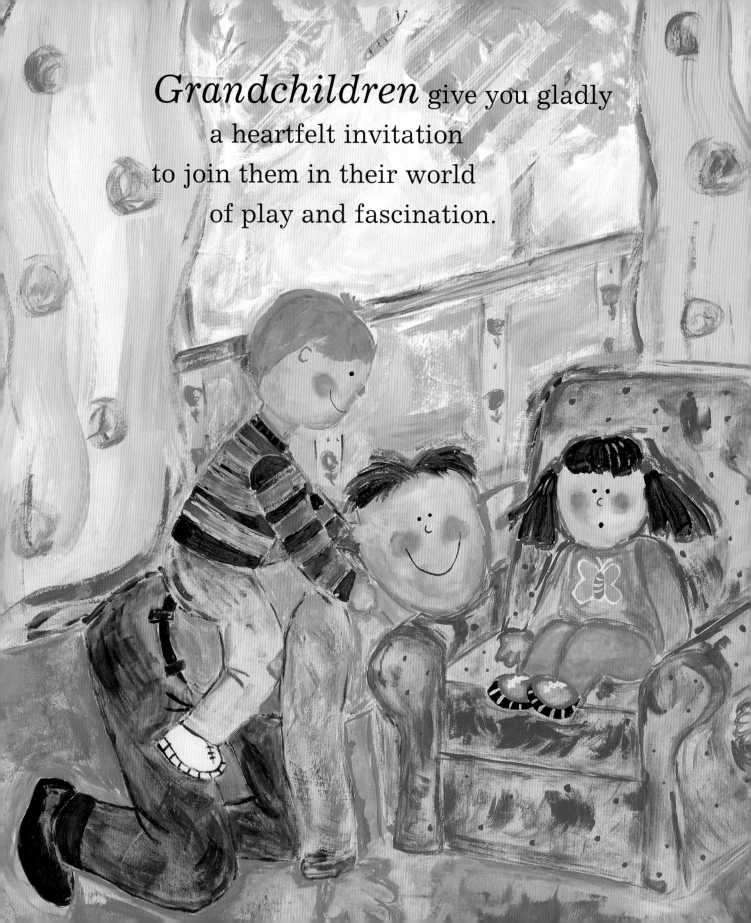

Grandchildren give you gladly
a heartfelt invitation
to join them in their world
of play and fascination.

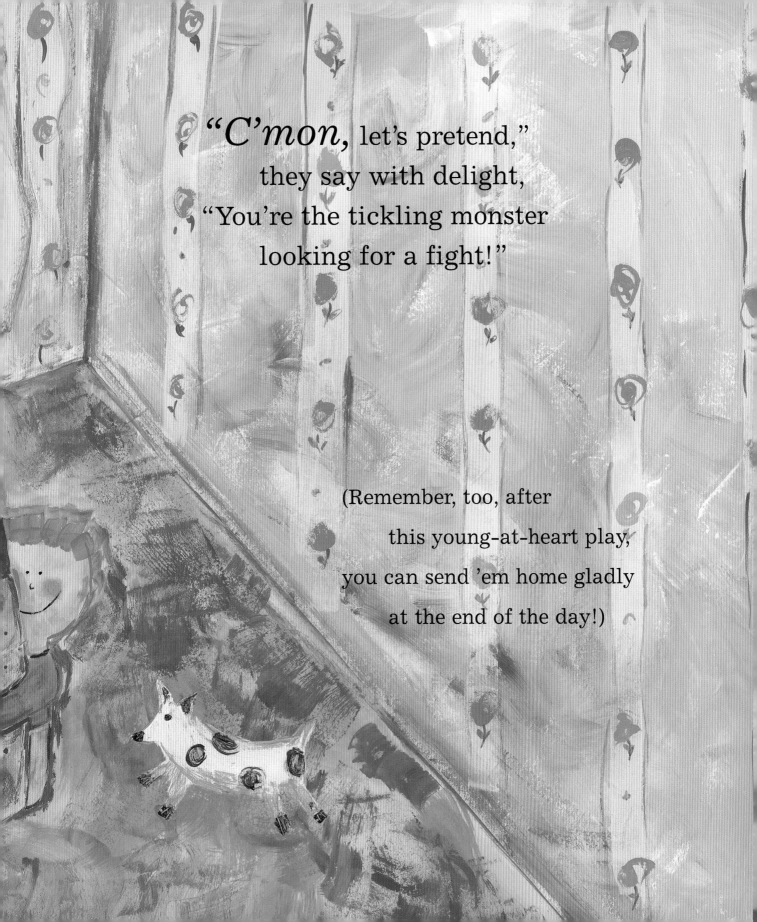

"*C'mon,* let's pretend,"
they say with delight,
"You're the tickling monster
looking for a fight!"

(Remember, too, after
this young-at-heart play,
you can send 'em home gladly
at the end of the day!)

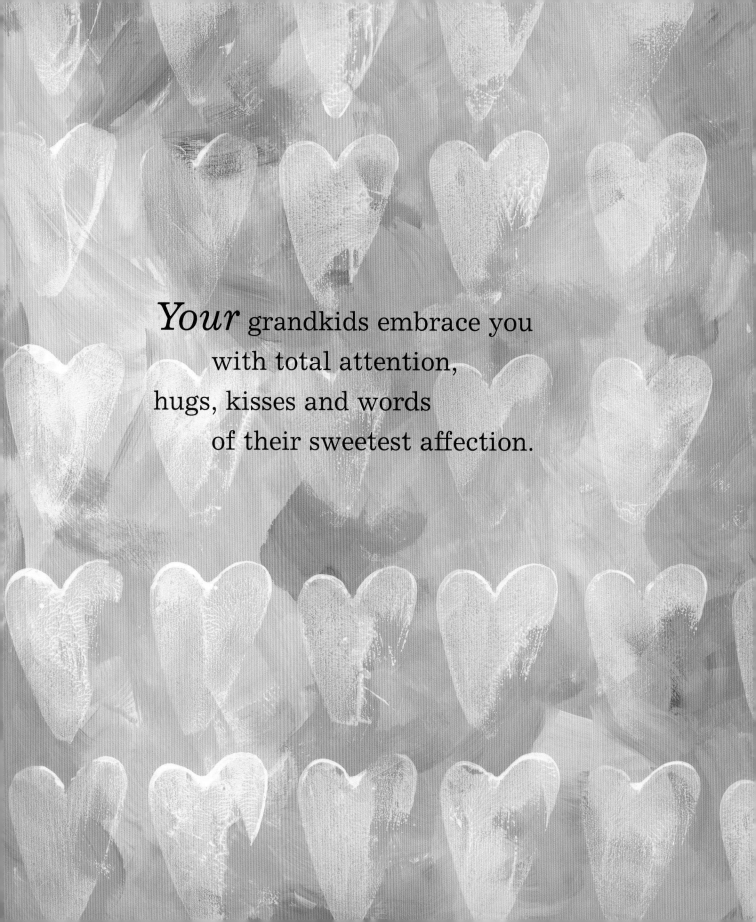

Your grandkids embrace you
with total attention,
hugs, kisses and words
of their sweetest affection.

They'll listen to stories
    of life way back when
their parents were kids
    and what happened then.

To you it seems like yesterday,
    the stories that you tell,
but these kids of your kids
    may have kids someday as well!

For now, just delight in this grand new stage
that comes when it does, no matter your age.

The best thing of all is the adventure unplanned
when life gives to you
the gifts of being grand!